ABOUT THE ALDEN ALL STARS

Nothing's more important to Woody, Derrick, Jesse, and Bannister than their team, the Alden Panthers. Whether the sport is basketball, hockey, baseball, or track and field, the four eighth-graders can always be found practicing, sweating, and giving their all. Sometimes the Panthers are on their way to a winning season, and sometimes the team can't do anything right. But no matter what, you can be sure the Alden All Stars are playing to win.

"This fast-paced [series] is sure to be a hit with young readers."   —*Publishers Weekly*

"Packed with play-by-play action and snappy dialogue, the text adeptly captures the [eighth-grade] sports scene."   —*Booklist*

Benched!

The *Alden All Stars* series:

ALDEN ALL STARS

Benched!

David Halecroft

PUFFIN BOOKS

PUFFIN BOOKS
Published by the Penguin Group
Viking Penguin, a division of Penguin Books USA Inc.,
375 Hudson Street, New York, New York 10014, U.S.A.
Penguin Books Ltd, 27 Wrights Lane, London W8 5TZ, England
Penguin Books Australia Ltd, Ringwood, Victoria, Australia
Penguin Books Canada Ltd, 10 Alcorn Avenue, Toronto, Ontario, Canada M4V 3B2
Penguin Books (N.Z.) Ltd, 182–190 Wairau Road, Auckland 10, New Zealand

Penguin Books Ltd, Registered Offices: Harmondsworth, Middlesex, England

First published in Puffin Books, 1992
1 3 5 7 9 10 8 6 4 2

LIBRARY OF CONGRESS CATALOGING-IN-PUBLICATION DATA
Halecroft, David.
Benched! / by David Halecroft.   p.   cm.—(Alden All Stars)
Summary: Woody and his friend Bannister work hard to make the
eighth-grade basketball team, but then they allow basketball to come
before everything else—including schoolwork.
ISBN 0-14-036038-7
[1. Basketball—Fiction. 2. Schools—Fiction.] I. Title.
II. Series.
PZ7.H13825Be 1992   [Fic]—dc20   91-31823

Printed in the United States
Set in Century Schoolbook

Benched!

1

"Ladies and gentlemen, the whole season comes down to this one single free throw," Woody Franklin said, talking in his fake sportscaster's voice. "The pressure is all on Franklin, the rookie from Cranbrook."

Woody put his right foot a half inch from the free-throw line, dribbled three times, then spun the basketball until the seams stopped against his fingertips. He stood perfectly still for a couple of seconds—knees bent, brown eyes gazing intently at

1

the back of the rim. Next, he took one deep breath. It was all part of Woody's new free-throw routine, and he wanted to get every part right.

When he was ready to shoot, he lifted his hands, thrust his body upward, and sent the ball sailing toward the basket. The ball dropped through the rim without touching it, and swished through the net with a snap.

"Woody Franklin has just sunk the championship-winning free throw," Woody shouted, "and the crowd is going absolutely nuts!"

The gym at Alden Junior High was quiet, except for the echo of Woody's voice and the squeak of his high-tops on the polished wooden floor. It was Saturday—the first day of try-outs for Alden's eighth grade basketball team—and Woody had come forty-five minutes early to practice shooting. Only a few lights shone in the empty gym, and the bleachers were lost in shadows. Woody liked the sounds of dribbling balls and squeaking shoes—because the sounds meant basketball. And basketball, for Woody, meant everything.

Woody was medium sized, with long lanky arms and legs, and quick brown eyes that darted around the court. Last year, playing guard on the seventh grade squad, he had been known as a smart play maker, and a strong defenseman who stuck to his man like glue. The only problem had been Woody's shooting. Although he had been great at setting up plays, his shooting percentage—from the outside and from the free-throw line—had left a lot to be desired. Coach Butler, the seventh grade coach, had told Woody that his shooting was the only thing keeping him from being a top-notch player.

Setting up at the free-throw line again, Woody smiled to himself. This season, things were going to be different. Woody had just spent his Christmas break at a basketball clinic, and he was psyched about the season. Woody's hero, Michael Jordan, had made a special appearance at the clinic. He had told the kids that as long as they worked hard, they could be as good at basketball as they wanted to be. That night Woody had laid wide awake in bed, planning how he would work and practice every day, just like Michael Jordan. Woody could feel it in his bones— this was his season to shine.

He set up at the line and went through each step in his free throw routine. He dribbled three times, spun the ball, and took a deep breath. When he was ready, he pushed up smoothly and released the ball.

Another swish.

"Yeeow-wow!" someone cried in the shadows, as soon as the ball swished through.

Woody recognized the scream. He grabbed the rebound and hurled the ball across court.

"Hey, Bannister," he called. "Heads up!"

Ed Bannister—whom everyone called by just his last name—snatched the ball after one bounce.

"Check it out, sports fans," Bannister said, running onto the court and chucking the ball as hard as he could. "Bannister tries a last-second shot from half court!"

The ball floated high up into the shadows, dropped, then banked off the backboard and blasted through the net.

"Unbelievable!" Woody cried, giving Bannister a high five as he jogged into the key.

Bannister was all smiles. "It's just part of the new me," Bannister said.

"The new you?" Woody asked.

"Just wait," Bannister said, grabbing the rebound. "You'll see."

Bannister was the class clown, a popular guy with a big gut and a great sense of humor. But, because he was overweight, Bannister had never excelled in sports. He had done a good job on the track team last

4

season, but that was in the shot put, where he didn't have to run. Whenever the track team ran their warm-up laps, Bannister had lagged far behind.

Even though Woody was glad to have Bannister around, he wondered why his friend was even bothering to try out for the basketball team. Bannister had a pretty good shot, that was true—but basketball was a running game, and Bannister was in terrible shape. Last winter Bannister had been cut from the seventh grade basketball squad, and Woody couldn't see a single reason for this season to be any different.

Bannister stood at the free-throw line, wearing a heavy gray sweat suit that bulged out around his stomach. Woody was already in his shorts and basketball shirt, his brown hair matted down with sweat. Bannister took a shot from the line, and the ball bounced off the rim.

"I know what *you* did over Christmas break," Bannister said, as Woody tossed him the rebound. "But I'll bet you can't guess what *I* did."

"I bet you sat around the house and ate Christmas cookies," Woody teased, as Bannister shot again.

"Hah!" Bannister said, launching the ball through the net. "Guess again."

"Whatever it was, you didn't learn how to shoot

from NBA players," Woody answered. He grabbed the ball, dribbled back around Bannister, faked forward, then went up for a fade-away jump shot. The ball banked off the backboard, rolled around the rim, then flew off into Bannister's hands.

"You're not Michael Jordan yet."

"Just give me time," Woody said.

"So did you do anything at that clinic besides play basketball?" Bannister asked.

"What else is there? Homework?" Woody chuckled and slapped at the ball.

"Well, for starters, there's Spanish," Bannister answered, dribbling toward the basket.

"Are you kidding?" Woody replied. "Working on Spanish isn't as much fun as shooting free throws."

"Yeah, but your Spanish grades were pretty bad last semester, in case you forgot," Bannister said, doing a sloppy lay-up. "*Muy terrible,* in fact. If you don't pick up your grades, you won't even be allowed to play."

"Oh, yeah?" Woody said, smiling. "And why are *you* so worried about basketball? You'll be watching the season from the bleachers anyway."

"Very funny, Wood-head," Bannister said. He was used to his friends teasing him. Bannister jerked his head up to the basket like he was going to shoot, and Woody looked up, too. But instead of shooting, Bannister whipped the ball at Woody, smacking him in the chest.

Bannister let out a howl of laughter and took off running.

"Very funny," Woody yelled, snatching the ball and taking off after Bannister.

Woody was surprised at how fast Bannister was running. It actually took Woody two laps around the gym to finally catch up, and plug Bannister with the basketball.

"Okay, men!" Coach Trilling called, five minutes later. Now the gym was bright with lights, and lots of boys were dribbling around and shooting. Coach blew his whistle. "Bring it in."

All the boys gathered in a half-circle around Coach Trilling. With a whistle around his neck, a clipboard in his hand, and an Alden baseball cap on his head, Coach had a reputation for working his players hard.

"I know most of you, and I've seen most of you play," Coach began. "But I want you to know something. This is a brand new season. No one is guaranteed a place on the team, not until I see what everyone can do. And remember, I give a lot of credit to players who hustle. OK, let's start off with some half-court wind sprints."

Woody lined up next to Bannister and Matt Greene. Matt had played forward last season, and he was by far the fastest player on the Panther squad. In fact, he held a conference track record in the 100-meter dash. Woody nudged Matt in the shoulder as they squatted down.

"Hey Matt, watch out for Bannister," Woody joked. "He told me he was going to cream you in the wind sprints."

"Uh-oh," Matt said, pretending to shake. "I'm really scared."

"If you think you're shaking now," Jesse Kissler said, crouching down next to Matt, "just wait until Bannister starts running. Then the whole *gym* will be shaking."

Bannister opened his mouth, but Coach blew the whistle before he could make a comeback. At the sound of the whistle, the players sprinted forward, running as fast as they could.

Woody watched Matt pull ahead of him on the first lap. He touched the center line, and sprinted back toward the basket. He couldn't catch up with Matt, and finished third—behind Matt and Bruce Judge.

Woody turned around to look for Bannister, expecting to find his friend huffing and puffing back from half court. But Bannister was standing right next to him.

"How did you get here so fast?" Woody asked.

"I ran," Bannister answered.

By the time they had finished four more wind sprints, everyone was looking at Bannister with amazed expressions. He had finished in the middle of the pack, ahead of Jesse, Chuck Lambert, and Chris Pesce. For Bannister, it was an incredible performance.

Bannister just stood there smiling, and didn't say a word.

Next, Coach had each player dribble to the basket and do a lay-up. Woody looked good, running fast and keeping his eyes on the basket as he dribbled. He jumped high, laid the ball against the backboard, and watched it drop through the net. Woody grabbed his own rebound and passed out to Matt.

Even though Matt ran faster than Woody, he glanced down at the ball as he dribbled. He jumped high and put the ball up, but it deflected off the rim and bounced to the floor. Matt snatched the ball and passed out to Bannister.

Bannister kept tight control of the ball as he

dribbled, holding his eyes on the basket. He jumped higher than Woody could believe that he could, and laid the ball into the hoop. The team clapped and cheered as Bannister grabbed the rebound, and made a sharp pass to the next player in line. Woody hadn't even expected Bannister to get off the ground.

When Coach called for a short break, Woody, Matt, and Bruce all rushed over to Bannister.

"It's the new all star!" Woody said, slapping Bannister on the shoulder. "But I can't figure it out. What happened?"

"Are you ready for a surprise?" Bannister said, smiling. He pulled off his sweat suit. Everyone's mouth dropped open as they stared at Bannister in his shorts and T-shirt.

"You've lost weight!" Matt said at last.

Bannister spun around, and everyone laughed and clapped. He wasn't exactly *thin,* but he wasn't fat anymore either.

"I've been on a diet since September," Bannister explained. "And I've been running and shooting hoops a lot. I'm going to keep right on losing weight—until I can run as fast as Matt."

"So what exactly *did* you do over Christmas break?" Woody asked.

"I went to a clinic, too." Bannister picked up a basketball and started to dribble. "Only at the one I went to we learned how to eat right. No more chips and pizza for me."

"I'll believe that when I see it," Bruce added.

"All right everyone," Coach called out. "Enough messing around. Let's get back to work."

On the way back to center court, Woody gave Bannister a high five. Woody *had* noticed that Bannister looked a little thinner this year. But he'd never imagined he'd gotten this fit. Woody was surprised, but he had to admit he was proud of Bannister.

During the shooting drills, Woody hit everything—jump shots, lay-ups, free throws. Suddenly, Woody seemed to be the best shooter on the team.

Bannister losing weight, and running fast? Woody hitting all his shots?

It looked like it was going to be a season of big surprises for the Alden Panthers.

2

Three days later, Coach posted the final Panther roster on the boys' locker-room door. Woody leaned in close to the list. He wanted to make sure he wasn't seeing things. Then he spun around and let out an ear-piercing victory yell.

Both he and Bannister had made the team.

"Hey, Bannister!" Woody shouted, speeding back down the hallway, nearly knocking down the custodian as he raced past.

"What's all the excitement about?" Bannister asked, trying to act like he wasn't nervous. "You're screaming like an old lady."

"Welcome to the Panthers," Woody said, punching his friend in the shoulder. "You made the team."

Bannister's eyes got big and round, and for a split second Woody was afraid that Bannister might keel over and faint. But then Bannister tossed his gym bag up into the air.

"I did it!" Bannister shouted, giving Woody a high five. "I did it! I'm a Panther!"

Woody hadn't been all that worried about making the team himself. He knew that his shooting had improved, and that he was still the best ball-handler on the team. But Bannister was a different story. Bannister had been fat and unathletic for so many years that it was hard to imagine him hitting the court in a Panther uniform.

"Hey, Bannister," Woody said, as they slipped on their practice clothes. "What do you say I give you some extra pointers and advice after practice? I know you made the team and everything, but I think you could still work a little on your shooting and dribbling."

"I like it!" Bannister said, his eyes lighting up.

"You could teach me everything you learned at the clinic."

"Yeah," Woody said, getting excited about the idea. "We could practice every night after dinner, in your driveway. We'll dominate the court."

Coach Trilling blew his whistle and called the eighth grade Panthers to attention. There were only twelve players on the court now—the final twelve who had made the cut. Woody and Eddie Peres would be first-string guards, Matt and Bruce Judge would be the forwards, and Jesse Kissler would be the center. Bannister would play on the second string team—as a forward—along with Chuck Lambert, Chris Pesce, John Buckner, and Matt Kindel. Everyone looked pumped up to play ball.

"Congratulations," Coach began, looking over the new Panther squad. "I think we can have an excellent team this year, but we'll have to work at the basics—dribbling, passing, shooting. We're not going to run a lot of fancy offenses, or a lot of fancy zone defenses. We'll have one basic offense—the high post. And one basic defense—the man to man."

Woody felt his heart sink in his chest. At the basketball clinic, he had worked on lots of different offenses and defenses—the "box and one" zone, the

14

low-low post offense. Now Coach was saying that they'd just run a man-to-man defense and one high-post offense. It didn't sound too exciting to Woody.

"Who can tell me what a high-post offense is?" Coach asked.

Jesse raised his hand. "It's when the center sets up as the post man in a high position, right around the free-throw line."

"Right," Coach said. "And what's a post man?"

Bruce spoke up. "The post man stands in the middle of the action, relaying passes, setting screens, and shooting. He's like the center of the play."

Woody knew that the high-post offense was used when the team's center was a quick player—quick enough to get in from the free-throw line for rebounds. But Alden's first-team center, Jesse, was not known for his speed. In fact, he was really slow, and had a funny, clumsy way of running. Since Jesse wasn't fast enough to make rebounds from a high-post position, that would put more pressure on Woody to crash the boards. That sounded good to Woody. He planned on being the star of the Panthers, and he knew he could handle the extra pressure.

After warming up with wind sprints and dribbling drills, Coach had the team work through some plays from the high-post offense. At the end of the day the team had two plays down, and Coach called for a half-court scrimmage.

Woody got the ball at half court, and charged forward, dribbling fast. John Buckner was playing him tight, so Woody passed in to Matt.

Matt grabbed the ball and held his ground just by the free-throw line. Woody ran past Jesse, the center—forcing John right into Jesse's side, and leaving Woody open. Matt pumped him a fast pass right beneath the basket. Woody dribbled once and jumped, banking the ball off the backboard and into the net for a perfect lay-up.

"Nice play," Coach called out. "Woody, way to use the pick. Let's try it again."

Woody was psyched. He had scored his first real basket as a member of the eighth grade team—even if it was only a lay-up. He couldn't wait until he got his first chance to take a jump shot. Then he could really show Coach Trilling how good he was.

Woody started out fast from midcourt, but John was playing him tight, shuffling along as Woody dribbled forward. Woody stopped, pivoted, and faked a pass to the left. When John lunged after the fake, Woody side-armed a bullet pass to Jesse at center, then took off running for the give and go.

He slid by Jesse, got open in the key, and Jesse threw a one-bounce pass. But Bannister—on defense—flared off his man and got a hand on the ball. It deflected across the key, and Matt snatched it up for Woody's team.

"Matt, over here!" Woody called out, running into the corner. "I'm open!"

Matt picked up his dribble, spun around, and chucked a pass to Woody. Woody could have dribbled forward, working his way closer to the net, but instead he sent the ball flying through the air for a long jump shot. He waited for the ball to swish through the net.

But it didn't even come close to the rim, and Woody's face turned bright red. Bannister snatched the rebound for the other team.

Coach blew the whistle.

"It's the air-ball king," Bannister teased, under his breath, as he tossed the ball back to Woody.

Woody tried to laugh and shrug it off, but his confidence had been shaken by his gigantic air ball. He knew he could have hit that shot in a shooting drill. But shooting drills didn't matter. What mattered was hitting the shots under game pressure.

"You should have charged the net, Woody," Coach

said. "That shot was too far out. Let's see some smart shooting out there."

But Woody didn't hit one jump shot for the rest of practice. If he shot one ball too short, then he'd shoot the next one too long. If he shot one ball off to the left, he'd shoot the next one off to the right. He looked like the old Woody Franklin—good dribbler, bad shooter. It was as if he'd never even been to the basketball clinic.

After dinner that night, Woody ran through the empty streets of Cranbrook. He was going over to Bannister's house to shoot hoops in the driveway. The air was chilly, and Woody was wearing two layers of sweat shirts and a blue knit hat. He tried to dribble his ball a few times as he ran, but the ball was too cold and it hardly bounced. That meant they couldn't really work on dribbling, but that was okay with Woody. He just wanted to work on his jump shot anyway.

The Bannisters had a wide driveway with a new basketball hoop mounted above the garage. Floodlights hung from the sides of the house, and lit up the backboard and the whole driveway, making it easy to practice at night. Bannister was already shooting lay-ups when Woody rushed up, bounding over a bush and shrieking into the middle of the driveway.

"Franklin from half court," Woody called out, roping in a pass from Bannister, "and there are only three seconds left in the game. Three, two, one. . . ." He chucked a wild shot toward the backboard—and swished it.

"Swish-master Woody!" Bannister shouted, grabbing the rebound. "Why couldn't you do that in the scrimmage today?"

"I choked," Woody answered, grabbing Bannister's pass and jumping up for a sky hook. The ball banked off the backboard, rolled around the rim, and dropped in for a basket. "But I don't plan to choke in the game next week."

"Speaking of next week," Bannister said, "have you started studying for the Spanish test yet?"

"Spanish?" Woody said, throwing his head back. "Who cares about Spanish?"

Bannister shrugged and threw a fade-away jumper. "You know, we have to get started on our science project or you'll fail science as well as Spanish," he said, picking up the ball.

"What I've got to do is practice my jump shot,"

Woody said, grabbing the ball from Bannister's hands.

Finally, after a half hour of shooting, Bannister made an incredibly long hook, then went inside to finish up his homework. But Woody stayed on practicing jump shots, until he was so tired that he walked home and fell right into bed.

3

Woody went up for the rebound, boxing out the St. Stephen's forward, and snatched the ball as it deflected off the rim. It was seconds after the tip-off in Alden's first conference game of the year, and Woody wanted to get the season off on the right foot.

"Woody, Woody!" Matt called out, running up the court alone.

Woody faked a pass, thew his defender off balance, then surged around him on the opposite side. He dribbled into open space, and looped a long pass to Matt.

It was a fast break.

Woody took off toward Alden's basket. He felt good about his first rebound of the season, but he knew he wouldn't relax until he'd hit his first outside shot. He'd been practicing hard all weekend in Bannister's driveway, and now was the time to prove that he could shoot and score under game pressure.

Matt went up for a fast break lay-up against a tall St. Stephen's player, but the ball deflected hard off the rim, and bounced over the defender's head.

It was a footrace to the loose ball—and Woody won, snatching the ball just above the key. He could have driven in closer to the net, but he wanted his first basket of the season from outside. He jumped high, aimed for the back of the rim, and launched the ball toward the basket.

Woody watched the ball bank off the backboard and power through the net, and heard the fans in the Alden Junior High gym let out a cheer.

"Yes!" Woody said under his breath, making a fist as he ran up court. Suddenly, he didn't feel nervous anymore. He felt loose and strong—and ready to cream St. Stephen's.

By the end of the first quarter, the score was Alden

14, St. Stephen's 7. Woody had already scored six points, all of them jump shots. St. Stephen's just didn't seem strong enough to stop the fast Panther offense, or the scrappy Panther defense. Coach had left the starters in for the whole quarter, so Bannister hadn't hit the floor yet. Woody hoped Bannister got a chance to play soon, before the Panthers pulled too far ahead and the game got sloppy.

"We're playing good ball, but let's keep alert," Coach said in the break before the second quarter. "Matt, try not to pick up your dribble too soon. Woody, nice shooting out there. Jesse, make sure to box out their center. Let's not underestimate St. Stephen's. This game is only one quarter old. Got it? Okay, let's play ball!"

Jesse won the tip-off, knocking the ball out to Eddie, who dribbled up court. Eddie passed the ball in to Jesse at center, and Woody took off down the left side of the key. Matt set a strong pick for Woody, knocking the defender down and leaving Woody open under the basket. Jesse whipped the ball to Woody, who went up for a left-handed lay-up.

Woody put too much spin on the ball and St. Stephen's got the rebound. He clapped his hands in frustration and ran up the court. It had been an easy lay-up, and he'd blown it.

Woody stuck close to his man. He wished Coach would let the Panthers run at least *one* zone defense—but if Coach wanted the team to play man to man, then Woody would do the best he could.

St. Stephen's was working from the high-post offense, the same one that the Panthers used. The St. Stephen's guard worked the ball in close to the basket, then passed off to Woody's man. Woody crouched down and shuffle-stepped with his man, swiping his hand to knock the ball away. His man made a strong move toward the basket and Woody lunged—only to watch the St. Stephen's player stop dead in his tracks and nail a perfect jump shot.

Woody started thinking that maybe Coach was right—maybe this game wasn't going to be so easy.

The Panthers missed their next three scoring opportunities. Suddenly the score was St. Stephen's 15, Alden 14. Either the Panthers were getting lazy, or defense and the momentum had quickly swung St. Stephen's way.

Woody grabbed the pass from Bruce at the top of the key and angled in toward the hoop, driving hard. He planted both feet, and opened up for a jumper. The shot missed again, hitting the side of the rim and dropping into Eddie's arms.

Eddie pivoted, ducking and faking, but he couldn't

get open so he passed back out to Woody. Woody wanted this shot, and he wanted it bad. He knew if he could hit a solid jumper, his confidence—and the team's confidence—would come back.

He put the shot up. It was a total air ball, and it landed right in the St. Stephen's center's hands. He made a fast pass up court, and a second later the St. Stephen's guard sunk an easy lay-up, bringing the score to 17–14.

That was when Coach decided to substitute Bannister for Bruce. Woody was psyched for Bannister, and gave his friend a high five as he came off the bench. Still, Woody couldn't figure out why Coach would put Bannister in when the team was falling behind, and needed its best players on the court.

Bannister clapped loudly as the Panthers set up beneath their own net. "Let's show these wimps what the Panthers are made of."

Bannister caught the pass in bounds and dribbled up court, moving slowly with his head up. He whipped a pass to Eddie, who was charging up the floor ahead of his defender.

"Let's go, Ed-man," Bannister shouted. "Come on, Panthers!"

Eddie stopped short and went up for a jumper, and the ball hit off the side of the rim. Bannister was there, boxing out his man for position. He jumped up for the rebound and snagged the ball.

"Bannister!" Woody yelled. "Kick it back!"

Bannister chucked a bounce pass to Woody, and Woody went up for the shot.

Swish!

"All right!" Bannister cheered, giving Woody a quick thumbs-up as the Panthers headed up the court. "Panthers!"

Woody smiled. The Panthers were coming back.

Coach only left Bannister in for four minutes, though, but that was long enough for the Panthers to regain the lead. When the second quarter ended, the score was Alden 24, St. Stephen's 19.

"Nice play out there," Woody said to Bannister at halftime. "You really got us psyched."

"Hey, every once in a while my loud mouth is good for something," Bannister answered, flicking his towel back at Woody. "You had a pretty good first half yourself. I guess all your extra practice is really paying off."

In the second half, the Panthers totally overpowered St. Stephen's. Woody sunk another three field goals, with Matt and Eddie sinking two each. Bannister got back into the game for a few minutes, but he missed a jump shot and ended the game without scoring his first point of the season.

When the final buzzer sounded, the Panthers had beaten St. Stephen's 46–30. And soon the locker room was filled with laughter and cheering—the sounds of victory.

After the game, Woody, Bannister, Bruce, and Matt went to Pete's Pizza to celebrate. Pete's was in the Cranbrook Mall, and on most afternoons there were lots of Alden kids hanging out there.

Woody led the boys to his favorite table, over by the windows with a view of the mall action, while Bannister picked up the pizza.

"A feast!" Bannister said a minute later, putting a large pepperoni pizza in the middle of the table. But he only put three paper plates down—one for Woody, one for Bruce, and one for Matt.

"Don't tell me you're not eating, Bannister," Bruce said, grabbing a slice and shoving it in his mouth.

"How do you think I lost all this weight?" Bannister asked, making a face at Bruce. "By chowing down on pepperoni pizza?"

"Oh come on, Bannister," Woody said, nudging his friend in the ribs. "You can have *one* slice."

"Okay, okay," Bannister said. He pulled one little piece of pepperoni from the pizza and held it up. It was about the size of a quarter. "I'll eat this pepperoni if it will make you guys happy. Here's to the Panthers!"

Bannister popped the pepperoni into his mouth. Then he reached into his jacket pocket and pulled out an apple and two rice cakes. Bannister took a huge bite out of the apple and smiled as he chewed.

"Hey, have you guys decided what you're going to do your big science project on?" Matt asked as he wolfed down a second slice.

Woody shrugged. He and Bannister still hadn't come up with any ideas for their big science project. Bannister had been bugging Woody about it, but Woody had had other things on his mind. Like getting ready for today's game. But now that today's game was over, it was time to start getting ready for the *next* game.

"Wood-head doesn't worry about school anymore," Bannister answered. "He's too busy getting ready for his NBA debut."

4

Woody boxed out the North Colby man and snagged the rebound as it bounced off the boards. He hunched down, protecting the ball, and waited for the floor to clear.

Woody was dominating the game.

It was halfway through the fourth quarter, and the score was Alden 31, North Colby 20. Woody had already racked up thirteen points, eight rebounds, and eight assists. If he ended the game with ten rebounds and ten assists, he would have made the first "triple double" of his life.

A defender was crowding him, waving his arms in his face. North Colby was running a full-court press, and the other Alden players were tightly covered.

"Woody!" Bruce shouted, getting open for a quick pass.

Woody faked a high pass, then whipped the ball low, right under the hands of the North Colby player. Bruce snatched the pass, and Woody burst past his defender. Since North Colby was on a full-court press, they didn't have anyone near the basket.

It was a perfect fast break situation.

Bruce crossed the center line, then hurled the ball to Woody like a quarterback. Woody snagged the pass—but by the time he got control, he was almost under the basket. He jumped fast, laid the ball on the backboard, then flew out of bounds. He was going so fast that he smashed into the pads on the wall of the North Colby gym, and crumpled to the ground.

But he heard the Alden bench cheering, and figured he must have made the shot.

"Air Woody!" Bannister said, helping Woody to his feet. "Great play."

As Woody hopped to his feet, he felt a jab of pain in his ankle. He must have twisted it when he hit the pad, and he limped a little when he tried to run.

"Woody?" Coach called out from the sidelines, ready to substitute Chuck Lambert. "Are you OK?"

"I'll just run it off, Coach," Woody answered, limping up court and getting set for defense. "I'm fine."

Woody was having his best game ever, and he wasn't about to sit the rest of it out. He was determined to get a triple double.

North Colby was working the ball around, trying to find an opening in the Panther defense. Woody was covering his man tight, keeping close enough to touch him. The ball was in the right corner of the court when Woody's man broke across the lane for a pass. Woody broke with him, but when he pushed off with his leg, he felt a jab of pain in his ankle. He slowed down and the North Colby man got open. The pass came in and the player grabbed it and went up for a jump shot.

"Come on," Woody said to himself, rushing the net for a rebound. "Just run it off."

The shot bounced hard off the rim, and Woody was in position for the rebound.

Woody laid back and waited as Eddie brought the ball up court. He knew he probably should take a break and give his ankle a rest. But with his ninth rebound he was too close to stop now.

Eddie tossed the ball to Woody at midcourt. Jesse was at the top of the key, waving for a pass. Woody dribbled around his defender, whipped Jesse a pass, and cut down court to set a pick for Bannister. He set up right behind Bannister's defender, and Bannister broke toward the basket.

The defender backed right into Woody, and Bannister was free. Jesse bounced a perfect pass to Bannister, and Bannister went up for a lay-up. His form was good, and he jumped higher than Woody had ever seen him jump. But the ball bounced off the backboard, traveled twice around the rim, then flew off. Woody charged in for the rebound, leaping high and pulling it out of the hands of a North Colby player.

"Good rebound!" Coach shouted from the bench. "Keep control of the ball. Set up another play."

It was Woody's tenth rebound. If he could get two more assists, he was golden.

Woody started dribbling back out, as if he were going to set up another play. But halfway up the key he saw Bannister cut toward the basket, all alone.

Woody spun around and chucked Bannister a bullet pass. Bannister stopped short, pumped a fake, then went up for a jumper.

The ball swished through the net.

"Yes!" Woody said, giving Bannister a big thumbs-up. Bannister had scored the first real basket of his life!

Not only that, but Woody had racked up another assist. One more, and he'd have his triple double.

Woody turned and ran down the court, still limping a little. His man caught a pass, and Woody tightened up his coverage. He shuffled along as fast as he could, swiping at the ball, and trying to block any possible passes. The North Colby player faked right and cut left—and left Woody in the dust. Woody tried to make up his lost ground, but his ankle slowed him down. He could only watch as the North Colby guard sank an easy lay-up.

Coach signaled for Bruce to call a time-out, and a moment later the referee blew his whistle. Woody knew what Coach had on his mind, and he didn't like it.

"Chuck, go in for Woody," Coach said, sending

Chuck over to the scorekeeper's table. "Woody, have a seat and give that ankle a rest."

"But Coach," Woody began, "if I get one more assist, I'll have a triple double. My ankle's fine."

"Sorry, Woody," Coach said, pointing at the bench. "You're too important to the team. Besides, we're ahead by fourteen points. We've got this game locked up."

Woody took a seat on the bench and shook his head. Even though he was disappointed, he couldn't help but be happy about the Panthers' performance. They had dominated North Colby all afternoon.

When the buzzer sounded, the score was Alden 40, North Colby 25.

"How's that ankle?" Bannister asked Woody, as they walked back toward the locker rooms.

"No problem," Woody answered. After resting it for a few minutes, Woody's ankle felt perfectly fine. Woody slapped Bannister on the back. "You looked great out there. I think our practice is really paying off. Your jump shot was perfect."

"A total swish," Bannister said, dunking his hand down. "And you almost made a triple double today."

"Yeah," Woody said. "Almost."

"You'll get it next time," Bannister said, opening up the locker-room door.

"You bet I will," Woody answered.

Woody took a bite of his hamburger—then another—until his cheeks were puffed out like a chipmunk's.

"You eat like a pig, Woody," his older sister Jill said, when they were at the dinner table that night. "It's embarrassing."

"I'm hungry," Woody answered, sending his sister a sharp look. "And I'm in a hurry."

"Where are you going?" Mrs. Franklin asked.

"It's Tuesday night, Mom," Woody said, swallowing. "Every Tuesday night is open gym night at school."

"What about schoolwork, Woody?" Mrs. Franklin asked, putting down her fork. "Don't you have a big science project coming up?"

"That's not due for another three weeks," Woody answered. "Besides, Bannister is my partner. He's great at science."

"That tub of lard?" Jill said. "Ha!"

Sometimes Jill made Woody so mad that he almost exploded.

"That's enough, Jill," Mrs. Franklin said. "Besides, he's lost a lot of weight."

"Yeah, you should have seen him in the game today," Woody said to Jill. "He nailed a jumper from fifteen feet, and he snagged at least three rebounds. And he sets a pick better than any forward on the team."

"You should have seen *Woody* in the game today," Mrs. Franklin said proudly, nodding across the table. "He was scoring baskets left and right."

"I almost got a triple double," Woody said. He looked up at his big sister. "You probably don't even know what one is, do you?"

Jill pretended that she didn't hear him, so she didn't have to answer. Woody smiled, and popped the last bite of hamburger in his mouth.

"What about your Spanish homework?" Mrs. Franklin asked. "Your grades have been pretty bad since the basketball season started."

"Bannister can help me with Spanish," Woody said, scooting out from the table. "He'll be at the gym tonight."

"Then why don't the two of you figure out your science project?" Mrs. Franklin asked. "You should get started on it."

"Okay," Woody said, snatching the ball from under his chair. "No problem."

He couldn't wait to hit the court again. The game that afternoon hadn't even tired him out. In fact, it had just gotten him more pumped up about basketball. The last thing he wanted to think about was schoolwork.

As he walked past his sister, he picked up the last piece of her hamburger and tossed it into his mouth.

"Very funny, Woody," his sister said. "If you keep that up, you'll end up looking like Bannister."

"You mean, like Bannister *used* to look," Woody said, heading toward the door. "Right now, Bannister is a lean, mean, fighting machine."

That night, he and Bannister worked on free throws in the junior high gym. Woody was too busy concentrating on his technique to ask Bannister about their Spanish homework. But Bannister brought up the topic of the science project. He wanted to build a mini-volcano—one that would erupt and spew molten lava all over the classroom. They could make a foldout display that showed how the volcano developed and the effects of its eruption on the atmosphere and surrounding ecosystem. It would take a lot of research and work, but Bannister seemed pretty excited about the idea.

"Yeah, yeah. Sounds good to me. Let's do some dribbling drills," Woody said, ignoring what Bannister was saying. "We only have a half hour left before the gym closes."

He dribbled a circle around Bannister, ran out to half court, and shot a giant sky hook.

"Yes!" Woody shouted, as the ball swished through the net.

5

"There are less than two minutes left in the game," Coach said, kneeling down on one knee. "Let's keep the pressure up. Full court press from now on. Okay?"

"Let's go Panthers!" Bannister called out from the bench. "We can beat these guys. Let's do it!"

Woody walked back onto the court, his hands on his hips. He had to admit, he was starting to get tired. He had played all but three minutes of the game, against a very tough Williamsport squad.

Williamsport was leading, 46–40. The Williamsport point guard—a strong, quick player named Mueller—was leading the league in scoring. He had played a great game so far, locking in his second triple double of the season. Woody was second in the league in scoring, but he still hadn't scored his first triple double.

But all he cared about was beating Williamsport.

Woody covered Mueller tight on the throw-in, nearly snagging the in-bounds pass. Mueller ripped the ball away and Williamsport was on its way down court.

Mueller passed to the center, then cut toward the basket for a give and go. Woody followed him into the key, until he saw Jesse steal the ball right out of the center's hands.

Woody turned around and sprinted up court. This was a crucial play. If they could sink a bucket now, they'd be within four points of Williamsport.

Jesse was being double-teamed, but he finally got the ball out to Bruce. Bruce dribbled up to center court and passed along to Woody. Mueller was taller than Woody, and had really long arms. Woody knew that if he went for a lay-up, Mueller would probably stuff the ball right back in his face.

Woody dribbled toward the basket, keeping an eye

out for open players. Eddie was just behind him, undefended, and Woody knew just what to do.

He jumped up for a lay-up, and Mueller jumped with him, ready to block the shot. Instead of putting the ball up, Woody swung a pass back to Eddie. Eddie snagged it and put up the shot. The ball banked through the hoop.

"Great play," Coach called from the sideline. "That's teamwork."

The Panthers were within four, with just over a minute left in the game. They slapped Williamsport with a full-court press, but Mueller still got the pass from out of bounds. Williamsport moved the ball up the court, and then got set up for the play.

Woody knew what was coming next—the stall.

Williamsport stayed in the backcourt, passing and dribbling, killing the clock. The Panthers were playing their tightest defense, trying to force Williamsport into a mistake.

"Go after the ball," Coach called from the sideline.

The clock ticked down, and Williamsport kept passing the ball back and forth. Things were getting desperate. Woody knew that if they didn't steal the ball soon, they'd have to foul a Williamsport player intentionally.

Woody saw a pass coming to Mueller, and took a

dive at the ball. He knocked the ball away, then tumbled to the floor. The ball went bouncing into the far court.

The Alden crowd was on its feet, cheering loudly.

Mueller tripped over Woody and fell onto the floor, and the two boys scrambled to their feet at the same time.

Woody pulled ahead and reached down with one hand to scoop up the loose ball. Mueller was breathing down his neck. His only chance was to try a lay-up against the taller player.

Woody leaped as high as he could, but Mueller jumped even higher. Woody got a shot off just before Mueller's arm came crashing down against his shoulder. The two boys fell in a heap beneath the basket, and both referees' whistles blew at once.

The crowd at Alden Junior High was going nuts.

Woody had sunk the basket and drawn a foul on the play as well. He was going to the free-throw line, to see if he could turn a lay-up into a three point play—and bring the Panthers within one point of Williamsport.

Woody put his right foot a half inch from the free-throw line. He dribbled three times, and spun the basketball until the seams stopped against his fingertips. Then he stood perfectly still for a couple of seconds, with his knees bent, just staring at the rim. His heart was pounding like crazy, but he tried to ignore it and concentrate on the free throw. After taking a deep breath, he thrust upward and released the ball with backspin.

Swish.

Woody clenched his fist, and ran forward for the full-court press.

The score was Williamsport 46, Alden 45 with fourteen seconds left on the clock. Alden didn't have a single time-out left, so all they could do was hope that Williamsport lost their cool.

Williamsport worked the ball toward the basket, then pulled back for the stall. The clock ticked down. Mueller passed the ball to the other Williamsport guard, who chucked it down to a forward. Bannister was tight on his man, swiping at the ball. The Williamsport player saw an opening and dribbled forward—right into Bannister. Bannister fell to the ground with a crash.

Whistles blew, and Woody's hopes rose.

"Charging, Williamsport, number fifty-three," the ref said. "One on one."

"All right!" Woody cheered. "You really drew that foul, Bannister."

"I'm a good actor, when I need to be," Bannister answered.

The Alden crowd was quiet as Bannister set up at the free-throw line. It was a one-on-one situation. If Bannister made the first free throw, he'd get to try a second.

And if he made the second one, the Panthers would probably win the game.

Woody lined up at the key. He watched Bannister dribble three times, then get ready to shoot. As soon as Bannister released the ball, Woody got ready for the rebound.

The ball bounced off the backboard, then swished through the net.

The crowd cheered, then got quiet again. The score was all tied up, with only four seconds left on the clock.

Bannister dribbled three times, then shot.

The ball bounced off the rim, hit the backboard, then bounced on the rim two more times before dropping through the net for a basket. Alden had taken the lead by one.

Williamsport grabbed the ball and took it out of bounds. They threw the ball in to Mueller, who took a half-court shot just as the buzzer went off.

Woody held his breath as he watched the ball fly

toward the basket. It seemed to take forever to come down. But finally the ball smashed against the rim, and flew up high into the air.

It landed on the floor—and the Panthers went crazy.

They had won.

"Bannister, you're a hero!" Woody cried, as he slapped Bannister on the shoulders.

"Just call me Mr. Clutch," Bannister answered, with a giant grin.

"A volcano is a hole in the earth's crust," Bannister said, closing his encyclopedia. "It shoots molten rock, and ash, and deadly gases miles into the air. Isn't that incredible?"

"Sounds boring to me," Woody answered, propping his chin up on his hand.

"Come on, Wood-head," Bannister said, crossing his arms. "We have to get started on this science project. *You* may not care about your grade, but *I* do."

"Okay, okay," Woody said. "What do we have to do?"

It was Saturday afternoon. Woody and Bannister were sitting in Bannister's family room, trying to get started on their science project. But Woody's eyes kept drifting away from the books. It was a warm day outside, with bright sun and a deep blue sky.

"First of all, let's write out a report on volcanoes," Bannister began. "Let's figure out exactly how they work. Then we have to figure out how to build one of our own."

Just then, Woody saw Jesse and Matt walking down the sidewalk. He jumped to his feet and ran toward Bannister's front door.

"Hey, where are you going?" Bannister called out.

"It's Jesse and Matt," Woody said, yanking open the door. "You up for a game of two on two?"

Bannister shook his head. When Woody Franklin got basketball on his mind, nothing else mattered. Bannister got to his feet and walked to the door.

Jesse and Matt were just coming home from working on *their* science project. They were almost finished building a small water distiller.

But Woody didn't want to hear about it.

"Let's play some hoops!" Woody called out, throwing a shot through Bannister's net.

6

"I'll bet you a pack of gum," Bannister said, wadding up his lunch bag.

"Deal," Woody answered. "Let's see you make the basket."

Bannister checked around for the vice principal, then jumped to his feet and tossed his lunch bag across the cafeteria. The bag slammed against the rim of the garbage can, spraying cookie crumbs all over the wall.

Woody laughed and held out his hand.

"Okay, okay," Bannister said, slapping the pack of bubble gum into Woody's palm. "I can't make *every* shot."

Woody, Bannister, Matt, and Jesse were having lunch in the cafeteria of Alden Junior High. The cafeteria was filled with chatter and the smell of school pizza. Bannister always used to say that lunch was his favorite class of the day. But nowadays, he was only eating things he brought from home.

"Hey, Bannister," Matt said, taking a bite of his sandwich, "how come you didn't finish your lunch?"

"My grandma is visiting and she keeps sneaking cookies in my lunch bag," Bannister said, shaking his head. "She just doesn't understand that I'm a superstar player now. I'm in training."

Everyone laughed. Bannister was no basketball superstar. He *was* improving, however. Woody thought that if Bannister kept losing weight, and kept working on his skills, he might even have a chance of replacing Bruce in the starting line-up.

"I remember when you used to eat all your lunch, even the bag and wrappers, and everybody else's too," Woody said, munching on a chip. He waved his bag of chips right under Bannister's nose. "Hey, Bannister, how about grabbing a handful?"

"Or a slice of pizza?" Jesse said, holding his pizza up to Bannister's face.

Bannister crossed his arms and kept his mouth shut. Finally, Woody and Jesse laughed and took the food away.

"Hey, how's your volcano project going?" Matt asked, grabbing Woody's bag of chips and helping himself.

"We haven't done a thing," Bannister answered. "All Wood-head wants to do is shoot hoops. And I don't feel like doing the whole project myself. If we don't start working soon, we're going to get a big fat F."

Woody wanted to change the subject. His grades had been getting worse and worse all semester. In fact, he had gotten a D on his last Spanish test. He usually did okay in English and math, if he crammed for the tests. But to do well in Spanish, you had to study every night—and Woody wasn't very good at that.

"Let's not talk about school," Woody said. "We've got more important things to worry about. Like beating Bradley today."

"Did you hear that Bradley played together in a winter league?" Matt asked. "They know a bunch of fancy plays."

"I heard that Bradley runs two different kinds of zones," Jesse said. "And they run a low-post *and* a high-post offense."

"Bradley is supposed to be good," Woody said, crumpling up his lunch bag. "But they haven't met the Panthers yet."

Woody tossed his bag across the cafeteria, and it slammed into the garbage can with a thud.

Woody picked up the loose ball. He put his shoulder down and tried to drive to the basket, but the Bradley player had him covered. Woody stopped, gave a head fake, then dribbled forward again—expecting his man to be left in the dust.

The defender stayed with him and Woody couldn't get near the basket. Finally he got a pass off to Jesse, who missed a shot from the foul line.

Bradley got the rebound, and Woody sprinted up court. He hadn't been able to sink a shot all game, and it was starting to get on his nerves.

The second quarter had just begun, and the score was Bradley 14, Alden 7. The Bradley squad was every bit as tough as people said they were. Woody was being covered by a blond-haired guy named Silver—one of the best defensemen Woody had ever played against. He wasn't a great scorer, but that didn't matter. If Silver could keep Woody from getting the ball in the hoop, Bradley would win the game.

Woody boxed out Silver, shoving him back from the boards, then leaped up and reached for the ball. He ripped the ball from a Bradley player's hands and landed with possession. The Bradley team fell back, and Woody felt his spirits rise.

He passed out to Eddie, who took the ball across center court. Eddie passed back to Woody, and Woody looked for an opening.

But Silver wasn't covering him anymore. Woody dribbled to his right, and saw a bunch of Bradley uniforms protecting the area inside the key. It was a zone defense, and Woody didn't know what to do. He had seen a lot of zones at his basketball clinic, but nothing like this.

"Woody!" Matt called out, coming out for a pass.

Woody sent Matt a bounce pass, and Silver was on it in a flash. He seemed to come out of nowhere to grab the ball. Woody turned and ran after Silver, but he wasn't fast enough.

Silver made the lay-up before Woody even reached the top of the key.

Coach called a time-out.

"Okay, Panthers, they're in a one-three-one zone," Coach said, bending down on one knee. "Don't let that confuse you. We need to keep running our offense, the same as ever. Now let's play heads-up ball out there. No more sloppy passes. Don't let Bradley psyche you out."

Woody took a deep breath. He didn't mind being second best in Spanish or science—but basketball was a different matter.

"Bannister, go in for Bruce," Coach said. "All right, Panthers, let's go!"

Woody and Bannister ran toward the Bradley net, to bring the ball in bounds.

"Hey Woody," Bannister said. "Let's try our famous ally-oop. We've got to do something to get the Panthers into this game."

Woody liked the idea. "Let's do it just like we always do," he said. "I'll pass to you, rush the net, and you get the ball to me when I'm already in the air."

"Just like Michael Jordan," Bannister said.

Bannister passed out to Woody, and Woody brought the ball up court. Bradley was still in a zone and Silver was playing under the boards. If he was going to score on the ally-oop, he'd have to get past Silver.

Woody whipped Bannister the pass, and broke toward the net. The ally-oop was all a matter of timing—perfect timing. He rushed into the key, and saw the Bradley defense come at him.

Woody leaped as high as he could, and turned to see Bannister's pass speeding at him. Silver just stood there, watching, as Woody snatched the pass and put the ball up. He landed on the court in perfect position for a rebound.

But he didn't need a rebound. The ball bounced around the rim, then fell through the hoop for two.

Woody slapped Bannister a high five and ran down the court. He had finally scored his first basket of the game. He was ready for more.

But Bradley had other plans. It seemed like the harder Woody played, the harder Bradley played, too. A few minutes later, Woody and Bannister tried another ally-oop—but Silver picked it off, dribbled the ball across the court, and sank an easy lay-up.

When the first half ended, the score was Bradley 26, Alden 14.

———

"We need to relax out there," Coach said in the locker room at halftime. "We need to play our own game, and stop letting Bradley psyche us out. The man-to-man defense works fine against Bradley's offense. Just remember to stick to your man."

Woody tried to stick to Silver, but Silver always seemed to get the upper hand. When Woody played Silver tight, Silver drove around him. When Woody played Silver loose, Silver went up for a jumper. It was the most frustrating game Woody had ever played.

And the most frustrating thing was that Woody knew he was *better* than Silver.

Woody drove down the baseline, dribbling low and protecting the ball with his shoulder. He passed over to Eddie, who took a jumper. Woody got into position for the rebound, boxing out Silver, then snatched the ball as it fell off the rim. He dribbled once, and powered up another shot from right beneath the basket.

The shot hit the rim and fell back down. Woody snatched the rebound and put it up again. But this time the ball bounced wide, and Woody scrambled for the rebound once again. He dribbled once and put the ball against the backboard—only to watch it roll off the rim and fall into Silver's hands.

"Three shots!" Woody said to himself in frustration.

Silver passed the ball over the center line, and a Bradley guard caught it and kicked across the key to the Bradley center. Woody could only watch as the center laid the ball into the hoop.

The score was Bradley 41, Alden 28, with two minutes left in the game. Matt had been playing well, racking up eight points so far. Eddie's total was six. Jesse and Bannister both had five.

Woody had scored only four points—his worst game this season.

With one minute left in the game, Woody grabbed a rebound under the Bradley net. He got the ball out to Eddie, who drove up court and set up the play.

Eddie passed to Jesse, then ran over to set a pick on Woody's man. Woody broke free and rushed toward the net, lifting his hand for a pass. Jesse bounced the ball to him, and Woody went up for a short jump shot, just inside the key. As he was letting the ball go, a Bradley player swiped him across the arm. The ball flew off the rim—but Woody was going to the line for two shots.

Woody put his right foot a half inch from the free-throw line and dribbled the ball three times. He spun the ball around, then stared at the back of the rim.

He shot, and watched the ball bounce off the rim, right into the ref's hands.

Woody could feel his face turning red with anger. What had happened to his game?

The ref tossed him the ball for his second free throw. Woody went through his routine, and tried to relax. He took a deep breath, and shot again.

The shot was low, and hit hard off the rim—so hard that Woody had a chance of getting a rebound. He leaped forward and ripped the ball right out of Silver's hands, then went up for a fade-away jumper. If he could only sink this shot, he would have made up for missing his free throws.

The ball went wide, and Silver grabbed the rebound. A few seconds later, the game ended with the score Bradley 44, Alden 30.

"Don't worry about it," Bannister said to Woody, on the bus-ride home. "Everyone has bad games."

Woody leaned against the window and watched the trees whiz by. He wondered what Michael Jordan would do in his situation. The bus passed by a playground, where a lone boy was shooting baskets. Woody turned his head, watching the boy hit one free throw after another.

"I've got to work harder on my basketball," Woody

said, hitting his fist against the bus seat. "That's what Michael Jordan would do."

"In my opinion, you've got to work harder at Spanish," Bannister said. "Otherwise, you won't even be able to *play* basketball. If you fail two tests, you're not allowed to play in any games."

"Coach would never keep me out of a game," Woody said. "The next time we play Bradley, I'm going to cream Silver."

7

Woody slammed his Spanish book shut, grabbed the miniature basketball from his desk, and set up near the bed for a sky hook. The hoop was mounted on his bedroom door, right above a huge poster of Michael Jordan.

"Franklin, with three seconds left," Woody said in his sportscaster's voice, chucking the ball. "Three, two, one. . . ."

The ball sailed over Woody's desk, hit the rim, and

bounced to the floor. Woody grabbed the rebound on the short-hop, and jammed the ball through the hoop. The rim shook and vibrated, and Woody raised his arms in triumph.

"Franklin is amazing, ladies and gentlemen," Woody said, running back for another shot. "He's only thirteen years old, and already he can slam dunk like Michael Jordan."

Woody had just gotten home from the Bradley game and was supposed to be studying for a Spanish test. It seemed that the harder he tried to concentrate on Spanish, the more he thought about basketball. In the game that afternoon, Silver had shown him up. Woody replayed every part of the game in his mind, trying to figure out what he would do differently next time.

"Silver is playing Franklin tight," Woody said to himself, "and Jesse Kissler is setting a pick."

In his mind's eye, he could see the floor at Bradley Junior High, and he could see Silver rolling off of Jesse's pick.

"Franklin drives toward the net, dodging through a hole in the Bradley defense," Woody said, dribbling across his bedroom floor. He faked left, drove right, faked a jumper, then jumped up to slam the ball.

Right then the door to his bedroom flew open—and Woody slam dunked the ball right onto his sister's foot.

"Woody!" Jill shouted, putting her hands on her hips. "I'm trying to study, and all I can hear is that stupid ball. Thud, thud, thud. You're driving me nuts!"

Woody bounced the ball a few more times. "C'mon, let's play a little one on one. Try to get the ball."

"Woody, I swear I'm going to . . . ," Jill answered.

"Calm down, you two," Mrs. Franklin said, stepping into the room. "Jill, go back into your room. Woody, I'd like to have a word with you."

Woody rolled his eyes, walked back to his desk, and slumped down in his chair. He knew what his mother was going to say. She was going to say that his grades weren't as good as they should be. And she also was going to say that basketball wasn't nearly as important as school.

The problem was, his mom didn't know a thing about basketball.

"That's a poster of Michael Jordan, isn't it?" his mother asked, sitting down on Woody's bed.

Woody nodded.

"Michael Jordan has the best moves of anyone in

basketball history," Mrs. Franklin said. "He can fly through the air for incredible slam dunks."

Woody was amazed. When did his mother start learning about Michael Jordan?

"If I were you, I'd want to be exactly like Michael Jordan," Mrs. Franklin continued.

"That's right," Woody answered, getting psyched. "I *do*. That's why I'm working so hard on my hoops."

"Good," Mrs. Franklin answered, crossing her arms. "And Michael Jordan also worked hard at *school*. He did well in high school, keeping a B plus average. And then he worked hard to graduate from college, too. He always says that school is the most important thing."

Woody didn't answer. He didn't think his mom had even *heard* of Michael Jordan.

"You have a big Spanish test tomorrow, Woody," Mrs. Franklin said, standing up from Woody's bed. "I don't want to hear any more dribbling or shooting tonight. I want you to hit those books."

As soon as his mother left, Woody sighed and opened up his Spanish book. He had done okay in Spanish in the fall. But now that the basketball season was under way, Spanish seemed like the most boring thing in the world.

"Mom told me I had to hit the books, didn't she?" Woody said to himself, breaking into a sly smile. "But she didn't say *which* books."

Woody put his Spanish book away and walked over to his bookshelf. He pulled out a book called *The Official NBA Action Book* and sat back down at his desk. He opened up the middle of the book, and started reading about all the best players in the league.

If he couldn't be playing basketball, at least he could be reading about it.

Woody looked at the first page of the test, and felt his heart sink.

He didn't know *any* of the answers.

Woody was in Spanish class, sitting at the back of the room, near the window that looked out over the playground. Mr. Fogle, the Spanish teacher, was sitting at his desk at the front of the room, keeping an eye on everyone.

Woody glanced through the rest of the test, took a guess at some questions, then looked over to Bannister's desk. Bannister was hard at work, staring straight down at the paper in front of him. So was Jesse, and so was Matt, and so was Bruce. Woody shook his head, sighed, and looked out the window.

A bunch of seventh graders were playing basketball on the playground. Woody propped his head up on the desk and watched someone hit a long fadeaway jumper. Soon, he was thinking about the game with Bradley again, and how he needed to work harder at his basic skills.

Before he knew it, Mr. Fogle told everyone to put their pencils down and pass the papers forward. Woody quickly tried to fill in some of the questions he had left blank, but he didn't have a clue.

"How'd you do?" Bannister asked, as the two friends headed toward the lunchroom. "I thought the test was pretty easy."

"Oh, I don't know," Woody answered with a shrug. "I didn't have enough time. I had to leave a bunch of questions blank."

"I'll bet you didn't study for one minute," Bannister said, nudging Woody in the side.

"Yes I did," Woody answered, breaking into a smile. "Exactly one minute."

Bannister laughed and shook his head. "Have you done any research on our science project? Time is running out, Wood-head."

"Relax," Woody said, opening up the door to the

lunchroom. "That's two weeks away. Besides, we have more important things to worry about. Like our game against South Colby."

"South Colby will be a piece of cake," Bannister said, pulling up a chair at their favorite table. "They've only won one game all season."

"I know," Woody answered, opening up his lunch bag. "But I want to be one hundred percent ready to play."

"All right, Woody," Coach Trilling said at practice the next day, "let's see you hit four out of four."

The whole team was standing around, clapping and chattering. Woody grabbed the pass from Eddie, and put up a jump shot from the side.

Swish.

He ran to the left side of the free-throw line and got another fast pass. He dribbled once and put it up.

Swish.

"Nice shot, Woody," Coach called out. "But don't dribble before you shoot. It just gives the defense time to get you."

Woody hustled over to the right side of the free-throw line, and put up another shot, this time without dribbling.

The ball banked off the backboard and powered

through the net. If he was this hot in the game tomorrow, South Colby didn't stand a chance.

He ran to the far side of the net, and put up his last shot.

Swish again.

"That's what I like," Coach Trilling said, clapping as Woody hustled back to the end of the line. "All right, Bannister, let's see it. Concentrate on putting the ball through the hoop."

As Bannister started his round of jump shots, someone rushed into the gym and told Coach that he had a phone call. Coach hurried through the door, and the Panthers kept on practicing.

Bannister's shooting was looking better than ever. He swished two of his shots, and just barely missed the other two.

"Nice shooting, Bannister," Woody said. "If you keep that up, you're going to make the starting lineup for sure."

Before Bannister could answer, Coach Trilling came back into the gym and blew his whistle. The drill stopped and the team looked at Coach.

"That's it for today, team," Coach said. "See you tomorrow. Woody, hang on for a second."

The team filed through the door, and Woody stayed behind, wondering what Coach wanted.

"That was Mr. Fogle on the phone, your Spanish teacher," Coach started. "He wanted me to know that you flunked today's Spanish test, and that your grades have been going downhill all semester."

Woody gulped.

"You're a good ball player, Woody," Coach went on. "You're the most important player on this team. But school comes first."

"I know, Coach," Woody said. "I was thinking so much about the Bradley game that I just couldn't study. I'll do better next time."

"I hope so," Coach said. "But until then, you're suspended from playing any conference games."

"What?" Woody asked, gasping. "You can't . . ."

"I'm sorry, Woody, but those are the rules," Coach said, turning around to leave. "You'll be on the bench for the game tomorrow. And you'll have to stay on the bench until your grades come up."

8

"I can't believe Coach suspended me," Woody said, sitting in the lunchroom the next day with Matt and Bannister. He had his arms crossed, and he hadn't even touched his lunch. "And all because I failed a lousy Spanish test."

Bannister shrugged his shoulders. "Like Coach said, those are the rules. And you can't say I didn't warn you."

"Well, I'll only miss one game," Woody said. "All

I have to do is get a C on the next Spanish quiz, and that's no problem."

"You should get Eddie to help you in Spanish," Matt said. "He speaks Spanish."

"No, I can do it on my own," Woody said. He picked up a potato chip and threw it in his mouth. "It's easy. All I have to do is cram for the tests."

"Come on, Wood-head," Bannister said. "You have to study Spanish every night. You can't just cram for a test and expect to do okay."

"I don't want to talk about Spanish anymore!" Woody said, throwing his bag of chips down. "Spanish, Spanish, Spanish! I can't believe I'm not allowed to play in the game today—and all because of a stupid *Spanish* test."

"Luckily we're playing South Colby," Matt said. "We should be able to beat them, no matter what."

Woody started to pack up his lunch, throwing a whole sandwich back into his bag. He was too angry to eat. He had worked hard to become the best player on the Panthers—and one of the best in the conference. And now he couldn't even play.

"Hey, Woody," Bannister said, grabbing Woody's lunch bag. "You're not going to throw that sandwich out, are you?"

"I'm not very hungry today," Woody answered.

Bannister pulled Woody's sandwich from the bag, and ate half of it in one huge bite.

"Bannister!" Woody said. "What about your diet?"

"I'm nervous," Bannister said, scarfing down the second half of Woody's sandwich. "And when I get nervous, I eat."

"What are you nervous about?" Matt asked. "We'll cream South Colby, no problem."

"It's not just South Colby," Bannister answered, eating Woody's potato chips, one after another. "I'm nervous about the whole season. With Woody off the team, we're going to have a tough time."

"Off the team?" Woody asked. "But I'll be back for the Lincoln game."

"Not if you don't do some schoolwork," Bannister said, pulling Woody's cookies from the bag and popping them into his mouth.

Woody watched Bannister eat the whole bag of cookies, and then stand in line to buy some more food. It was just like the old Bannister.

That afternoon, Woody watched the South Colby game from the Panther bench. South Colby had a weak defense, and Woody thought about all the baskets he could have been making. But he *wasn't* making any baskets—he was riding the pine. It was the most frustrating thing in the world.

Especially when the Panthers started losing.

"I don't know what's wrong out there, Coach," Matt said, during a time-out. The game was almost over, and the score was South Colby 34, Alden 29. "We just can't seem to get any plays started."

"These guys have the worst defense in the conference," Coach began, looking around at his players. "We should be creaming them. The problem is, we're taking too many long jumpers. Remember, there's no three-point shot in junior-high basketball. So drive the ball toward the basket."

"Hey, Coach," Bannister said, as the players hit the floor again. "Why can't Woody just come in and play?"

"Yeah," Matt said, "South Colby doesn't know that Woody flunked a Spanish test."

Woody's hopes rose. He leaned forward so he could hear Coach's answer.

"I wish I could put Woody in," Coach said. "But the rules are the rules. Even though it's hard for you guys to believe, school really *is* more important than a basketball game."

Woody slumped down, shaking his head. This game, the Panthers were on their own.

He watched the Panthers take the ball out of bounds, underneath the South Colby basket. Eddie got the pass and dribbled across center court. He set up for a play, then charged forward toward the basket.

The South Colby players reacted quickly, closing their zone. Eddie leaped into the air, spun around, and tried a lay-up—but he was rejected by the tall South Colby center. Woody knew that he could have made the shot himself, but all he could do was clap his hands together to cheer on his teammates. He watched the ball deflect off Jesse's leg, and roll toward Bannister.

Bannister snatched the loose ball and went up for a long jumper. His form was perfect—a high jump and a strong shot—but the ball didn't even hit the rim.

"Air ball!" the South Colby fans shouted. "Air ball, air ball!"

South Colby got the rebound and worked the ball up court. The guard hit a fade-away jumper from fifteen feet, to bring the score to 36–29.

Woody was starting to think that the Panthers didn't have a chance against South Colby. They had been playing catch-up ball all game, and had never gotten the momentum to swing their way.

Bannister took the ball out of bounds, and passed in to Eddie. Eddie headed up the court, faking out one defender, out-dribbling another, then getting into an all-out foot race with the South Colby guard. They were running neck and neck toward the basket.

Eddie faked a right-handed lay-up, then twisted around for a reverse. It was a great play, and the ball dropped through the net.

"All right, Eddie!" Woody shouted, jumping to his feet and clapping. For the first time all game, he felt that the Panthers might have a chance. If Eddie could pull off a few more plays like that, the momentum might swing in the Panthers' direction.

The South Colby guard drove hard, working the ball toward the net. But when the guard had taken two steps, Matt darted past him, snatched the ball in mid-dribble, and started down the floor in a fast break.

Woody yelled from the bench, "Come on, Matt! Get the ball in the hoop!"

Matt checked behind him, saw a South Colby guard breathing down his neck, and stopped short.

The guard tried to stop and change direction, too, but Matt had enough time to sink an easy bank shot.

Woody clapped and looked up at the scoreboard. The score was 36–33—and there were only thirty-five seconds left in the game. He coudn't believe that a game between the Alden Panthers and South Colby was coming down to the wire.

"Let's go, Panthers!" Woody shouted. "Come on, let's see another steal!"

Bannister was having the worst game of his season. He had blown at least seven easy scoring opportunities, missed a bunch of rebounds, and made some bad passes. Woody hoped Bannister didn't get too down—because when Bannister got bummed, the whole team got bummed.

The South Colby center put up a shot, and Jesse grabbed the rebound. The clock was ticking down—twenty-four, twenty-three, twenty-two. Jesse passed out to Eddie, and Eddie took the ball up court. He set up a play, then passed the ball in to Bannister.

Bannister grabbed the pass and went up for a shot.

"Air ball, air ball!" the South Colby crowd shouted, as the ball fell toward the basket.

It *was* an air ball—but the shot ended up landing right in Eddie's hands. Eddie dribbled once, then went up for a bank shot. On the way up, he was fouled by South Colby. The ball sank through the net just as the referees sounded their whistles.

"Yes!" Woody said, leaping to his feet.

Eddie stood at the free-throw line. The score was now South Colby 36, Alden 35. Woody loved shooting the shots that really mattered, and he wished *he* were on the free-throw line.

Eddie dribbled, set, and shot. The Panther fans erupted into applause as the ball dropped through the net, to tie up the game.

The clock was down to ten seconds, and South Colby charged forward toward the basket. Alden slapped them with the heaviest defense of the game, and Bruce ended up stealing the ball with only four seconds left. Bruce passed the ball out to Matt, who was running up court.

It was a fast break. When the timer reached one, Matt laid the ball up and into the basket.

The buzzer rang, and the Panthers had pulled off an incredible last-minute victory.

Woody leaped to his feet and hit the court. The whole team was crowding around giving each other high fives and cheering.

Woody was psyched that the Panthers had won.

Still, he couldn't help but wish that *he* had been the hero of the game.

Sitting on the bench during such a close game was torture.

Later that afternoon, Woody, Bannister, Eddie, and Matt were at Pete's. Bannister was pigging out, cramming his fifth slice of pizza into his mouth.

"It's the old Bannister," Woody said, shaking his head. "You're going to turn into a blimp again, if you keep that up."

"I had the worst game of my life today," Bannister said, taking another bite. "We should have beaten South Colby by twenty points. And if it weren't for some incredible plays down the line, we probably would have *lost* to South Colby."

"We really need you out on the court, Woody," Eddie said.

"Don't worry," Woody answered. "I'll be back for the Lincoln game."

"You better be," Matt said, taking a sip of his soda. "Lincoln's a tough team."

"Hey, I hear there's a Spanish quiz the day after tomorrow," Eddie said. Eddie was taking French, but he tutored a lot of his friends who took Spanish.

"You better study for it, Woody. I could help, if you want."

"Yeah, Wood-head," Bannister added, shoving another piece of pizza in his mouth. "You better study."

"Relax," Woody answered with a shrug. "If I cram a little tonight, I'll get a C on the quiz for sure."

9

Woody was in the middle of a reverse dunk when the phone rang. He slammed the ball through the hoop, and then ran to the phone.

"Hello?" Woody said, still a little out of breath.

"Why are you breathing so hard?" the voice on the phone said. "You're supposed to be studying for your Spanish quiz, not playing hoops."

Woody smiled and sat down at his desk. "Hey, Bannister. I was just taking a little study break, that's all."

"I hope it's a *little* study break," Bannister answered. "Just remember, we play Lincoln on Wednesday. And we need you on the floor, not on the bench."

"Okay, okay," Woody answered, dribbling the ball on his desk. "I'll get back to the books."

"Don't forget about our science project, either," Bannister said. "After the game, we should get together and really work on our volcano."

"Wednesday night?" Woody said, putting his feet up on his desk and leaning back. "But Wednesday night is open gym night. We should get together and work on our shooting, not on our volcano. Don't forget, Bannister, you didn't have a very good game against South Colby."

Woody took a shot at the hoop. The ball banked off the ceiling and swished through the net.

"I don't want to talk about it," Bannister said. "I just want you to get a C on that stupid Spanish quiz, so you can play in the Lincoln game."

"Don't worry," Woody said. "I'm going to start studying as soon as you get off the phone."

"Do you promise, Wood-head?" Bannister asked.

"Promise," Woody answered.

As soon as Woody hung up the phone, he pulled his Spanish book from his knapsack and laid it on the desk. He opened up the book and turned the pages until he found the vocabulary section. After reading for five minutes, Woody yawned, stretched, and slammed his book shut.

"Time for a magazine break," he said, yanking open his desk drawer.

He pulled out a copy of *Sports Illustrated* and turned to a story on Michael Jordan. The article said that Jordan was one of the best basketball players ever. He could do things on the court like no one else—like jumping from the middle of the key, twisting around in the air, and doing a backward slam dunk. And yet, Jordan still worked on the basics, like his free-throw shooting.

"I have to be totally ready for the Lincoln game on Wednesday," Woody said, standing up and grabbing the ball from the floor. "And I'd better work on my free-throw shooting."

Woody stood back from his bedroom door, dribbled three times, and shot. The ball bounced off the rim and Woody rushed in for the rebound. He did a monster slam dunk, then dribbled back out for another free throw.

After forty-five minutes of shooting, Woody was hitting his free throws one after the other.

Right before bed Woody picked up his Spanish

book again. He quickly read through the exercises and vocabulary that would be covered on the quiz. After studying for a few minutes, Woody began to fall asleep. He shut the book and got into bed. He'd barely studied, but he was sure the quiz would be a piece of cake.

That Wednesday, the Panthers were in the locker room at Alden Junior High, getting ready for the Lincoln game.

The Spanish quiz had been the day before. Mr. Fogle hadn't given out the grades yet, but Woody thought he'd done okay. He couldn't wait to hit the court again, and lead the Panthers to victory.

"Hey, Woody," Jesse said, as the boys slipped on their blue and gold warm-ups, "has Mr. Fogle told Coach your grade?"

"Not yet," Woody answered, shrugging. "But don't worry, I'll be out there on the court today."

Woody led the team onto the floor, and they started to warm up. They did lay-ups first, then jump shots—and Woody felt great. He was hitting everything he shot.

"Let's go, Panthers," Woody shouted, clapping as the team ran through a lay-up drill.

The team looked pumped up. Everyone was running hard, dribbling fast, and hitting their lay-ups one after the other. Woody clapped and whistled, cheering the Panthers on. There was no doubt that Woody was the leader of the team. When he was playing well, things fell into place.

Just before the game started, Coach Trilling called the team together for a last minute talk.

"There's been a change in the starting line-up," Coach began. "Today, we're starting Eddie, Jesse, Matt, Bruce, and John."

Woody's heart stood still. Why had he been taken off the starting line-up?

"Woody will be on the bench again today," Coach went on.

Woody gulped, but didn't say anything.

"Nice going, Wood-head," Bannister said, shaking his head as he took a seat on the bench. "I guess Spanish wasn't as easy as you thought."

"It doesn't matter how good you are," Bruce said, sending Woody an angry glance, "if you're not allowed to play in any games."

"Next time, you'd better study," Eddie said.

Woody slumped down on the bench. He was so embarrassed about being benched that he didn't even think he'd be able to cheer.

Lincoln tore into the Panthers at the tip-off, and

all Woody could do was watch. The Lincoln squad won possession, then passed the ball quickly up court. Before Alden had a chance to set up their man to man, Lincoln drove the ball into the key and scored on an easy shot. Woody could tell that the Panthers weren't playing anywhere near one hundred percent.

Eddie set up the play for the Panthers. He passed to Jesse, then ran over to set a pick for Matt. Matt broke free and Jesse threw the ball in his direction.

The pass was wide and Matt dived for it, but a Lincoln guard snatched the ball away at the last second. He was halfway to the basket before Matt picked himself off the floor and lumbered toward the action. The Lincoln guard scored on a wide open lay-up.

"Come on," Eddie said, trying to get the team to concentrate. "Let's play Panther ball."

Eddie worked the ball up court, then passed off to Bruce in the corner. Bruce dribbled toward the basket, then chucked a one-bounce pass to John—who was breaking fast through the middle of the key. John fumbled the pass, but still tried to go up for a lay-up. A Lincoln player stripped the ball right out of John's hands, and the Panthers had blown another scoring opportunity.

Woody tried to clap and cheer, but it didn't feel right. He could tell that the team was angry at him. He didn't blame them, either. It really wasn't that hard to spend a half hour every night studying Spanish.

By the time the first quarter was over, the score was Lincoln 15, Alden 4. After that, Woody didn't even think about cheering. He could tell that the game was a lost cause.

In the second quarter, Jesse hit an inside jumper—then Eddie stole the ball in a full-court press and scored on a lay-up. Woody thought that the Panthers were on a roll, like the one against South Colby. But the Panthers' hearts just weren't in the effort.

Bannister only hit one shot all afternoon, and only got two rebounds. Jesse's passing was sloppy throughout the game—and since Jesse was the high-post man, that meant that the Panthers had a tough time making their plays work. Bruce played sloppy defense, allowing the fast Lincoln forward to drive to the hoop for basket after basket.

The final score was Lincoln 43, Alden 27.

It was a miserable game for the Alden Panthers.

After the game that afternoon, Woody was standing by himself in the locker room. He didn't feel like talking to anyone and the locker room was quiet in defeat.

"Bradley hasn't lost a game this season," Bannister said, tying his shoes. "They're going to make it to the championships, no matter what."

"But if *we* lose one more game this season," Bruce added, "we won't have a *chance* of making it to the championships."

"We just have to make sure we win the rest of our games," Eddie said.

Bannister, Bruce, and Eddie looked over at Woody.

Woody turned around and faced his friends. "All right, you guys. I promise I'll study hard. I'm going to get a B on the next Spanish quiz."

"You said that about the *last* Spanish quiz," Bannister said. "And then you ended up shooting hoops all night in your bedroom."

"And getting a D," Bruce said.

"Okay, okay," Woody said. "I've been stupid. But I'm going to make it up to the team. As long as Eddie helps me with my Spanish, my grades will be fine."

Eddie broke into a smile. "I'll come over to your house this afternoon, and we'll get started."

"Good," Woody said. "But we have to work fast. Bannister and I have plans for tonight."

"No way, Woody," Bannister said, shaking his head. "I'm not going to the open gym. I don't care how bad my shooting was in the game today."

"Who said anything about the open gym?" Woody answered, smiling. "Tonight, we have to get to work on our volcano!"

10

Woody and Bannister were sitting in Bannister's room, trying to make a volcano.

"We're never going to be able to finish this project in time," Bannister said, pasting a strip of sticky newspaper onto an empty bottle. They were trying to make a papier mâché volcano, but things weren't going so well.

"There's just too much to do," Bannister went on, dipping another strip of newspaper into a pot of flour and water. "We might as well just give up and get an F on the project."

"Then *both* of us will get suspended from the team," Woody said. "We can do anything—including making an awesome volcano."

"Wood-head, we have to do more than build a volcano. We have to have diagrams that show the earth's core and shifting of the continents. And we have to research how the eruption changes the areas around the volcano," Bannister explained.

"Huh?" Woody asked staring at his friend.

Bannister shook his head and pasted another strip onto the bottle. Then he wiped his hands off on a paper towel.

"I don't know about you," he said, "but I'm taking a snack break."

Bannister opened up a bag of chips and started munching—one chip after another—until half the bag was gone. Woody just leaned back and watched, shaking his head. Bannister had lost a lot of weight, worked hard, and become a good basketball player. Now it looked like Bannister wanted to throw it all away.

Woody decided that he'd seen enough.

"Give me those chips," Woody said at last, snatching the bag out of Bannister's hands.

"Hey . . ." Bannister exclaimed, surprised. "Give them back."

"If *I* have to study every day, then *you* have to go back on your diet," Woody said. "It's only fair. Besides, if you keep eating this way, you're going to be too fat to play in the championships."

"Who says we're going to make it to the championships?" Bannister asked. "We just lost to Lincoln."

"*I* say," Woody answered. "And not only that, but I'm going to get a B on the next Spanish test. And we're going to make the best volcano Alden Junior High has ever seen. We'll make it so it spews molten lava all over science class."

Woody made the sound of an erupting volcano, then screamed and pretended he was being covered in red-hot lava. He twisted around on the floor until Bannister cracked up.

"Are you sure you want to keep working on our volcano?" Bannister asked, raising one eyebrow. "Don't forget, it *is* open gym night. We could hurry to the gym right now and pick up a game of hoops."

"Let's go," Woody said. He grabbed Bannister's hand and dunked it in the pot of glue. "Just kidding. We'll shoot a round after we're done with our project."

Bannister looked at Woody and smiled. "I was only testing you, anyway," he said.

Woody picked up the bag of chips, "Don't you want to finish off the rest of these potato chips?"

"Forget it," Bannister said. "If *you* can stay away from open gym to work on our project, then *I* can stay on my diet."

Woody smiled and tossed the chips to the side of the room.

"Congratulations, Woody," Coach said before the North Colby game. He held up Woody's Spanish test and smiled. "You got a B minus. It's good to have you back on the floor. We've got a tough game today against North Colby."

"I'm ready for it, Coach," Woody said. "I can't wait to play again. Especially against that kid Mueller. I'm going to show him a thing or two about basketball."

Mueller, the star of the North Colby team, was still leading the conference in scoring. He had already earned three triple doubles this season. Woody still hadn't earned his first.

Woody remembered the game when he had almost gotten his first triple double. If Coach hadn't taken him out off the court at the last minute—because of a twisted ankle—Woody was sure he would have gotten his triple double. He was sure he was as good as Mueller.

Coach cleared his throat and banged a locker door. Everyone got quiet.

"We have two games left, men," Coach said, looking around at the team. "If we win them both, we go to the championship against Bradley. We've had some problems this season, but I still think we have the best team in the conference. We should be able to beat North Colby. So let's get out there and do it!"

The Panthers cheered, slapped each other high fives, and jogged onto the North Colby court for their warm-up drills.

Woody pumped a fake pass, then went up for a fade-away jumper. The ball swished through the net.

Woody drove hard past Mueller, dribbling low and keeping his head up. He did a reverse lay-up, nailing the shot.

Jesse side-armed a pass as Woody cut across the key. Woody grabbed the ball, stopped short, and hit a ten-foot jumper.

It had been like that all game—Woody was beating Mueller and hitting every shot he tried. He was also passing like a demon, and ripping rebounds off the boards. By the time the fourth quarter was coming to a close, Woody was well on his way to his first triple double. He had sixteen points, ten assists, and eight rebounds.

He wasn't even worried about the game anymore. The Panthers had come out strong, jumping to an early lead that had stunned North Colby. With less than one minute left in the game, the score was Alden 44, North Colby 30.

Woody was having the time of his life.

"Bannister, I'm open!" Woody called out, rushing to help Bannister, who had gotten trapped near the sideline.

Bannister passed to Woody, but the ball was wide. Woody put both toes at the edge of the sideline and leaned over to grab the ball. When he caught it, however, he felt himself begin to fall out of bounds. So he spun around and whipped a sidearm pass to Eddie, then dropped into the Panther bench.

"Nice footwork, Woody," Coach said, helping Woody to his feet and pushing him back onto the court.

Woody rushed back into the action. Eddie was dribbling around the key, looking for a hole in the defense. Woody saw him go up for a jump shot, then boxed out Mueller for position under the boards.

Eddie's shot slammed off the backboard, deflected off the rim, and flew into the court. Woody timed his jump, stretched his hand as high as it would go, and pulled down the ball for his ninth rebound. As Woody leaped to put the ball back up, Mueller smacked him across the wrist and the referee's whistle sounded.

Woody looked up at the clock. There were only four seconds left.

It was a one-on-one situation. Woody stepped up to the free-throw line, dribbled the ball three times, and gazed at the rim. He tried to concentrate on the shot, but all he could think about was getting his tenth rebound. He wasn't about to let this chance slip by.

He shot the ball and watched it bounce up off the rim. It hit the backboard, bounced off the rim again, then finally dropped through the net for a basket.

If he made his next free throw, North Colby would get the ball and the clock would die before they had a chance to shoot. If that happened, Woody wouldn't make his triple double.

Since the score was Alden 47, North Colby 33, there was no danger of losing the game.

In this situation, Woody figured there was only one thing left to do.

He got ready for the shot, spinning the ball in his hands. He thrust upward and whipped the ball low—right at the rim. Then he charged into the key, leaped up, and jumped for the ball as it hit the rim and deflected back.

Woody snagged his own rebound, dribbled once, and went up for a shot.

The ball fell through the net just as the buzzer sounded for the end of the game.

"Yes!" Woody shouted, clapping his hands and giving Bannister a high five.

"Congratulations," Bannister said with a smile.

Woody grabbed his towel and led the team to the locker rooms.

"I don't usually like my players doing trick free throws," Coach said to Woody, as the team hit the showers. "But I'm glad you finally got your triple double. Good work, Woody."

"Okay, Panthers!" Bannister called out. "Let's take it all the way to the championships."

That sounded pretty good to Woody.

11

Woody and Bannister set their volcano on the table, right at the front of the class. They had taped charts and displays on the blackboard behind them. Mrs. Fricke, the science teacher, sat down in Woody's seat.

"You two are the teachers for now," Mrs. Fricke said. "So teach us everything we need to know about volcanoes."

The volcano itself looked pretty good. It was a big

brown papier mâché mountain with a little hole at the top. Woody had done a lot of the research for the project, and had gotten together all of the ingredients they needed to make the volcano erupt. Bannister, on the other hand, had spent most of his time making a tiny village out of matchbooks. The village sat at the bottom of the volcano, with a little schoolhouse, some stores, and a few white houses.

Woody and Bannister explained the evolution of volcanoes first, using a cutaway picture Bannister had drawn of the earth's core. They talked about the volcano's effects—how it not only causes incredible damage to the villages that surround it, but how it also changes the earth's atmosphere.

Then Woody pointed at the mountain in front of him. "This is a volcano."

"And this is the town of Bradley," Bannister said, pointing at the little village.

The whole class broke out in laughter. Everyone knew that the Panthers were hoping to face Bradley in the championship.

"Bradley used to be a huge town," Bannister went on. "But it got smaller and smaller as time went by, because people were afraid of the giant volcano. They knew that, at any moment, the awesome power of the volcano could erupt—and sweep them off the face of the earth."

"By the way," Woody added, "the name of this volcano is Panther Mountain."

The whole class laughed.

"Panther Mountain sits on a place where the earth's crust is weak," Woody said. "The crater on top of Panther Mountain is a hole that goes straight down into the middle of the earth. Sometimes, all the molten rock and poisonous gases that are trapped inside the earth break free, and come shooting up out of the crater."

"That's an eruption," Bannister said, "And *that's* what we're going to do today."

"Is this going to make a mess, boys?" Mrs. Fricke asked.

"No, Mrs. Fricke," Bannister answered, trying to sound very serious. "Woody has it all figured out."

Woody had already filled the bottle with most of the ingredients. He had put some dishwashing soap in first, so the eruption would have lots of bubbles. Then he had added some red food coloring, so the eruption would look like molten lava. Next he put vinegar and warm water into the bottle.

"I have some baking soda in here," Woody said, holding up a big clear test tube. "When I add it to the volcano, it should combine with the vinegar and water—and then erupt."

"Are you sure this is going to work?" Bannister muttered under his breath. "I think we should add more soap and vinegar."

"No way," Woody whispered. "If we do that, the eruption will be too big."

"Too big?" Bannister laughed, as he poured more soap and vinegar into the crater. "You can *never* get too big."

Woody rolled his eyes and shook his head. This was a typical Bannister move—to do something crazy at the very last minute.

"It was a normal day in the town of Bradley," Bannister began, stepping back from the volcano. "The people were going about their business, when they noticed white smoke coming from the top of Panther Mountain. They had seen the smoke many times before, and nothing had ever happened. But today, it meant that Panther Mountain was about to erupt, and send hot molten lava through the streets of their quiet village."

Bannister paused as Woody dumped the whole test tube of baking soda into the crater. Then they both jumped back from the table.

KABOOM!

The lava exploded from the volcano, and a long stream of red foam flew straight up and hit the ceiling. Woody dived back against the blackboard, his mouth hanging open in amazement. Mrs. Fricke jumped to her feet, too, but there was nothing either of them could do. The volcano kept erupting and erupting, until half of the room was filled with red soap bubbles.

"And so, Panther Mountain erupted, and destroyed the village of Bradley," Bannister said, popping a bubble that hung in front of his nose. "And that's the end of our science project."

The whole class cheered as they watched the volcano die down. Even Mrs. Fricke couldn't help smiling.

It was the end of the regular season, and Bannister had not started in a single game. Coach Trilling wanted to keep the same starting five, game after game. In Woody's opinion, Bannister deserved to replace Bruce in the starting line-up. Bannister had worked harder than almost anyone on the Panther squad. He had gone back on his diet, and hadn't eaten an extra potato chip in days.

"I'm going to play as hard as I can today," Bannister said, just before the game. "And I'm going to show Coach that I have what it takes to start."

"I can help," Woody answered. "As long as we're winning and you're hitting your shots, I'll get the ball to you as often as I can."

Late in the first quarter, Bannister hit the floor and the Panthers caught fire. The score was Alden 18, St. Stephen's 9. Bannister was ready to put some goals in the hoop for Alden—and Woody was ready to help him.

"Woody, over here!" Bannister called, breaking free of his man and rushing toward the net.

Woody tossed Bannister a perfect pass. Bannister snagged it, dribbled once, and went up for a jump shot.

Swish.

As St. Stephen's ran up the floor, Bannister cut back, surprised the St. Stephen's guard, and stole the ball away with a quick jab of his hands.

He was all alone. He dribbled like a pro, keeping his head up and the ball low. At just the right moment, he leaped up and laid the ball off the backboard right into the basket.

The Alden crowd cheered and stamped their feet against the bleachers.

"Nice steal, Bannister!" Coach called out from the bench. "Keep it up!"

St. Stephen's brought the ball quickly into shooting range. Their point guard stopped short, pumped a fake, then went up for a fade-away jumper.

Woody spun around, crouched down, and boxed out the St. Stephen's guard. The shot went off the rim and Woody pulled it down. He looked around the floor for a breakaway pass.

"Woody!" Bannister shouted, running up the court.

Woody hurled a long pass, but it wasn't quite long enough. Bannister had to slow down to snag it, giving St. Stephen's time to catch up. Woody sprinted up the court, outrunning the St. Stephen's defense, and Bannister whipped him a beautiful pass just as Woody entered the top of the key.

Woody grabbed the ball, dribbled once, and went up for a lay-up.

The ball banked off the backboard and fell through the net. Woody clenched his fist and ran over to Bannister.

"Nice assist," Woody said, slapping Bannister's hand.

"Nice hoop," Bannister answered, smiling.

As they were running back to get into position, Bannister made a little motion with his hand. Woody knew exactly what Bannister meant. It was their secret signal for the ally-oop. Woody smiled and gave Bannister a thumbs-up.

Jesse grabbed the St. Stephen's rebound, and flipped the ball to Eddie, who worked it up court. Eddie dribbled to the foul line and passed to Woody. Woody dribbled around, setting up the ally-oop.

Bannister broke free of his man, and Woody passed the ball to him. Woody cut toward the basket, using Jesse to screen his defender. When he got close enough, he leaped into the air and looked over toward Bannister.

The pass was right there and Woody snatched the ball out of midair and put the shot up. By the time he hit the floor, the ball had already dropped through the hoop for two.

"Ally-oop, ally-oop!" the Panther crowd began to chant.

By the start of the fourth quarter, Woody was sure the Panthers had won. He was having another great game and was starting to really believe that he was as good as anyone in the league—as good as Mueller or Silver. Woody was also psyched for Bannister, who was playing the game of his life.

With ten seconds left on the clock, Woody nabbed a rebound under the St. Stephen's basket. St. Stephen's slapped on a tough full-court press. Woody twisted around, looking for a way to get rid of the ball.

The clock kept ticking down, and still nobody was open.

Finally, with three seconds left on the clock, Woody chucked the ball as far as he could at Alden's basket.

Bannister ran under the ball, caught it, and turned around to heave a half-court shot just as the buzzer sounded.

The ball traveled in a high arc, then powered off the backboard and through the net.

"Yes!" Woody said jumping up and running over to Bannister. "Amazing shot!"

The crowd was cheering and stamping their feet. All of the Panthers were on the court, slapping each other high fives. The scoreboard read Alden 52, St. Stephen's 40.

The Panthers were on their way to the championship.

12

"The starting line-up this afternoon is Eddie at point guard, Woody at shooting guard, and Jesse at center," Coach Trilling began, just before the start of the championship game. "Matt will be at left forward, and Bannister at right forward."

Woody looked over to Bannister and gave him a thumbs-up. Bannister was beaming with pride. He had shown Coach Trilling what he could do, and he had finally made the starting line-up.

Not only that, but he had made the starting line-up for the *championship* game.

"Bradley is a tough team," Coach went on, looking down at his clipboard. The visitors' locker room at Bradley Junior High was quiet. "We lost to them earlier this season. But that was a long time ago, and this team has learned a lot since then. Today, let's play good hard defense, get to the basket, and fight for rebounds. If we do that, Bradley will have their first defeat of the year."

The Panthers made a tight circle in the locker room, putting all their hands in the middle.

"One, two, three . . . WIN!" the team shouted, breaking their hands and charging out to the basketball court.

The gym at Bradley Junior High was crowded with fans. One side of the court was totally Bradley, the other side was totally Alden. The Bradley squad wore fancy sweat suits, and did their lay-up drills in perfect formation. The Panthers just wore their regular blue and gold uniforms, and looked loose and a bit sloppy as they did their drills. That was okay with Woody. It wasn't the warm-up drills that mattered.

During warm-ups, Woody kept an eye on Silver, the star Bradley guard. Silver was quick. He had shut Woody out in their last game together, with his tight, scrappy defense and quick moves. But Woody had worked hard at his basketball since the last Bradley game.

It was time to find out whether he'd worked hard enough.

Jesse lost the tip-off, and Bradley scored quickly with a jump shot from near the free-throw line.

Eddie took the ball out of bounds for the Panthers. He passed in to Jesse, who forwarded a pass to Woody.

Woody didn't feel like waiting for the Panthers to get ready for a play. He wanted to get the rally going *now*. So while the Panthers were still hustling down the court, Woody charged the basket—cutting and dribbling through a web of Bradley defenders.

Woody felt good today, loose and quick. He faked left, cut right, and went up for a quick lay-up. He imagined the roar of the Alden crowd as he sunk the first amazing basket of the game.

But just when Woody was about to put the ball up, Silver swooped in from the side and stripped the ball right out of his hands. Woody landed empty handed and looked over to the referee.

"Come on, Ref," Woody yelled as he ran up the court. "That was a foul if I've ever seen one."

Inside, Woody knew that Silver's steal had been clean. Still, he wanted to get the referee thinking— so that next time, he might make the call in Woody's favor.

Woody watched Silver pass the ball to the Bradley center. The center put up an easy lay-up for Bradley's second basket, and the Panthers were behind by four.

"Let's go, Panthers," Coach said from the sideline. "Let's jump back."

Right then, Bradley slapped the Panthers with a full-court press. Woody was surprised. Most teams only used full-court presses later in the game, so their players wouldn't get tired early on.

Eddie had the ball in the back court, trying to get over the line before the ref counted ten seconds. The offense needed to clear midcourt or they'd be called for a violation, but Bradley's press was good, and Eddie couldn't find anyone to pass to. He pivoted frantically, looking for an opening as the seconds ticked by. Woody was scrambling around the court, trying to get open, but Silver kept right on him.

Just when the referee was about to blow the whistle for a ten-second violation and give the ball back to Bradley, Eddie threw a long desperate pass. Bannister and the Bradley forward both tipped the ball, sending it bounding toward the Panther basket.

Bannister spun around and charged after the loose ball. He scooped it up and started dribbling, with the Bradley player breathing right down his neck.

"Come on, Bannister," Woody muttered, as he ran toward the action. "Get us on the board."

Bannister jumped, pumped a fake lay-up, then dished the ball off to Matt, who had broken free of his man. Matt went up and released a high jump shot off the backboard. The ball dropped through the net and the Alden crowd erupted with applause.

"Let's go, Panthers!" Bannister said, rushing back toward the Bradley net. "We can take these guys!"

Woody knew they could take Bradley, too. Still, he never felt right about a game until he made his first basket. And he wanted that to be as soon as possible.

Silver passed to the Bradley forward, then rushed toward the basket. Woody knew that the center would be right at the edge of the key, waiting to screen him as Silver flashed by. Woody rolled off the screen, then dodged forward in time to intercept the pass that was headed right for Silver's hands. Woody kept up his momentum, dribbling the ball as fast as he could. His brown hair was streaming out behind him, and his eyes were fixed on the Panther basket.

Woody did a left-handed lay-up, and the ball dropped through for his first basket.

The score was all tied up, 4–4.

When the first half ended, the score was still tied, at 27 all.

Woody had never been so exhausted in all his life. The Panthers had been running a full-court press for most of the second half, and Woody hadn't had a chance to catch his breath. During a time-out, Coach asked him if he wanted to take a break—but Woody said no. He might be tired, but he didn't want to miss a single chance to score a hoop for the Panthers.

Especially now, when there was less than a minute left in the championship game.

Silver was at the free-throw line. Woody bent over and rested his palms on his knees, breathing hard. He looked up at the scoreboard—Bradley 40, Alden 38. If Silver made this free throw, Bradley would move ahead by three. With less than a minute left, that extra free-throw point could mean everything.

Silver hoisted the ball up, and Woody got ready to jump for the rebound. When the shot hit the rim, Woody leaped into the key, boxed out the Bradley defense, and prepared to snag the ball. But the ball made a crazy bounce off the rim, and flew over Woody's hand. Silver snatched his own rebound, dribbled once, and went up for a fade-away jumper.

Woody leaped as high as he could to try and block the shot—but he couldn't leap high enough. The jumper swished through the basket, to put the Panthers behind by four.

There were thirty-two seconds left on the clock, and the Panthers didn't have a time-out left.

Woody caught the pass in from out of bounds and worked the ball up court. Silver was playing him as tight as ever, and Woody knew that he had to break free. He passed the ball to Matt, then rushed forward toward the top of the key—hoping to screen Silver off on Jesse.

It worked—but just for a split second. Matt passed in to Woody and Woody drove toward the basket. Silver spun off of Jesse's screen and stuck right to Woody's back. When Woody went up for a lay-up, Silver jumped with him.

The ball fell through the net, and the referee's whistle sounded.

"Foul on Bradley," the ref called. "The basket is good. Alden has one free throw."

Woody clapped his hands and clenched his fist. He could hear the Alden crowd going crazy. The clock was stopped at twenty-four seconds. If Woody could sink this free throw, the Panthers would only be one point behind.

He dribbled three times and took a deep breath. He tried to concentrate on the rim. Still, he couldn't help hearing the horns and screams and claps of the Bradley fans, who were trying to distract him. He dribbled three times again.

As soon as the ball left his hands, Woody knew that the shot was wide. The ball hit the backboard and deflected off the rim, and Bradley got the rebound.

The clock hit eighteen seconds and Bradley drove the ball up court. The Panthers were playing the tightest defense they had ever played. They were behind by two, and needed to get the ball.

But Bradley was stalling. They kept passing the ball back and forth, running the clock down. When there were only eight seconds left on the clock, Silver made a last drive toward the basket. Woody stopped him just outside the key, and Silver went up for a jumper.

Woody spun around, hoping the shot would miss. The ball hit off the backboard, traveled twice around the rim, then flew off into Woody's hands.

The clock showed four seconds. Woody looked around desperately for someone to pass to. Finally he saw Bannister running up ahead, and heaved the ball.

Bannister caught the ball at midcourt. He dribbled once, took a step, and threw the ball with one hand— just as the buzzer sounded.

The whole gym was silent as the ball traveled through the air. Woody thought that the ball would never come down. But it looked like a good shot, a *really* good shot. It got closer and closer. . . .

Swish!

The Alden crowd erupted into applause, cheering and clapping and pounding its feet.

Bannister had sunk an incredible half-court shot.

But it wasn't time to celebrate yet. The score was tied, and the game was going into overtime.

During the overtime period the score seesawed back and forth. Neither team led by more than a basket. With only twelve seconds left on the clock, Bradley was ahead by two points.

Bradley had the ball, and they were working it in

toward the basket. Woody kept an eye on the clock. He knew that if the clock got down too far, he'd have to foul a Bradley player intentionally, just so the Panthers could get possession of the ball again. The problem was, that would allow Bradley to go to the line, and pull ahead by three.

Silver cut in toward the basket and Woody saw his opportunity. The pass was a little sloppy and Woody dived for it. He knocked the ball out of the way, and fell to the floor.

Eddie hustled and gained possession, with eight seconds left on the clock.

Woody jumped to his feet and sprinted down the court. Eddie dribbled across the center line, getting heavy coverage from Bradley. Silver was right on Woody's back, but Eddie tried a long pass anyway.

Woody saw the pass coming and sped up. He jumped up as high as he could, and snatched the ball right out of Silver's hands. Then he took off running through the key.

"Three, two . . ." the crowd chanted.

Woody went up for a desperation shot, only to feel Silver's arm crush down against his shoulder. Woody hit the floor, heard the buzzer sound, and looked up at the basket.

The ball traveled three times around the rim, before it finally dropped through.

The Alden crowd went crazy. The scoreboard read Bradley 48, Alden 48, with no time left on the clock.

But Woody was allowed to shoot his free throw. If he made it, the Panthers were conference champions. If he missed it, the game would go into double overtime.

Woody stepped up to the line. He remembered his last free throw. He had gotten nervous and shot the ball wide.

"Just relax, Woody," Bannister said. "All you have to do is put that ball through the hoop. You've done it a million times before. Let the ball shoot itself."

Woody nodded. He dribbled three times, then spun the ball in his hands until he felt the seams stop against his fingertips. Since there was no time left on the clock, no one was set up around the key for the rebound. It was just Woody and the basket. He looked up at the rim, and took a deep breath.

Woody shot the ball, and felt his heart stand still.

The ball didn't even touch the rim. It swished

through the net—and the Panthers were the conference champs.

Woody raised his arm in victory and let out a giant banshee cry.

He had done it!

Bannister lifted Woody off the ground, and the entire gym exploded with the sound of cheering.